CHILDREN'S THRIFT CLASSICS

Alice in Wonderland

LEWIS CARROLL

Adapted by Bob Blaisdell
Illustrated by Marty Noble

DOVER PUBLICATIONS, INC.
Mineola, New York

DOVER CHILDREN'S THRIFT CLASSICS
EDITOR OF THIS VOLUME: JILL JARNOW

Published in Canada by General Publishing Company, Ltd., 30 Lesmill Road, Don Mills, Toronto, Ontario.
Published in the United Kingdom by Constable and Company, Ltd., 3 The Lanchesters, 162–164 Fulham Palace Road, London W6 9ER.

Bibliographical Note

This Dover edition, first published in 1998, is a new abridgement, by Bob Blaisdell, of the work first published as *Alice's Adventures in Wonderland* by the Macmillan Company, New York, in 1898 (the book was first published in 1865). The illustrations, by Marty Noble, the introductory note, and the footnotes have been specially prepared for this edition.

Library of Congress Cataloging-in-Publication Data

Carroll, Lewis, 1832–1898.
    [Alice's adventures in Wonderland]
    Alice in Wonderland / Lewis Carroll ; adapted by Bob Blaisdell ; illustrated by Marty Noble.
        p.   cm.
    "This Dover edition, first published in 1998, is a new abridgement . . . of the work first published as Alice's adventures in Wonderland by the Macmillan Company, New York, in 1898 . . ."
    Summary: A little girl falls down a rabbit hole and discovers a world of nonsensical and amusing characters.
    ISBN 0-486-40345-9
    [1. Fantasy.]   I. Blaisdell, Robert.   II. Noble, Marty, 1948–   ill.   III. Title.
PZ7.C2349335A1   1998
[Fic]—dc21   98-8401
                                                                                    CIP
                                                                                    AC

Manufactured in the United States of America
Dover Publications, Inc., 31 East 2nd Street, Mineola, N.Y. 11501

Note

LEWIS CARROLL, born Charles Lutwidge Dodgson (1832–1898), was an English mathematician and ordained deacon who loved to tell whimsical stories to children. At a time when children's books were grim and stuffy, he created *Alice's Adventures in Wonderland,* forever changing the style and content of children's literature. A unique combination of nonsense and fantasy, *Alice's Adventures in Wonderland,* which appeals to readers of all ages, is considered a masterpiece of English literature.

Titled *Alice's Adventures Underground,* the first version was hand written and illustrated by Carroll in 1862 as a gift to young Alice Liddell, for whom (with her sisters) he often improvised fairy tales. Henry Kingsley, a novelist, read the manuscript by chance during a visit to the Liddell home, and urged Mrs. Liddell to persuade the author to publish it. Adding further adventures to the story, and commissioning *Punch* magazine cartoonist John Tenniel to create illustrations, in 1865 Carroll brought out the first edition of *Alice's Adventures in Wonderland.*

Its popularity grew slowly. At Carroll's death in 1898, it had become the most popular children's book in England. By 1932, the centennial of Carroll's birth, it had become one of the most famous children's books in the world.

Contents

1. Down the Rabbit-Hole

Alice was beginning to get very tired of sitting by her sister on the bank and of having nothing to do: once or twice she had peeped into the book her sister was reading, but it had no pictures in it, "and what is the use of a book," thought Alice, "without pictures?"

So she was considering whether the pleasure of making a daisy-chain would be worth the trouble of getting up and picking the daisies, when suddenly a White Rabbit with pink eyes ran close by her.

There was nothing so *very* remarkable in that; nor did Alice think it so *very* much out of the way to hear the Rabbit say to itself "Oh dear! Oh dear! I shall be too late!"; but, when the Rabbit actually *took a watch out of its waistcoat-pocket,* and looked at it, and then hurried on, Alice started to her feet, for it flashed across her mind that she had never before seen a rabbit with either a waistcoat-pocket, or a watch to take out of it, and burning with curiosity, she ran across the field after it, and was just in time to see it pop down a large rabbit-hole under the hedge.

In another moment down went Alice after it, never once considering how in the world she was to get out again.

The rabbit-hole went straight on like a tunnel for some way, and then dipped suddenly down, so suddenly that Alice had not a moment to think about stopping herself before she found herself falling down what seemed to be a very deep well.

The Rabbit actually took a watch out of its waistcoat-pocket,
and looked at it, and then hurried on.

Either the well was very deep, or she fell very slowly,
for she had plenty of time as she went down to look
about her, and to wonder what was going to happen
next. First, she tried to look down and make out what
she was coming to, but it was too dark to see anything:
then she looked at the sides of the well, and noticed
that they were filled with cupboards and bookshelves:
here and there she saw maps and pictures hung upon
pegs. She took down a jar from one of the shelves as
she passed: it was labelled "ORANGE MARMALADE,"
but to her great disappointment it was empty: she did
not want to drop the jar, for fear of hitting somebody
underneath, so managed to put it into one of the cupboards as she fell past it.

"Well!" thought Alice to herself. "After such a fall as this, I shall think nothing of tumbling downstairs! How brave they'll all think me at home! Why, I wouldn't say anything about it, even if I fell off the top of the house!"

Down, down, down. Would the fall *never* come to an end? "I wonder how many miles I've fallen by this time?" she said aloud. "I must be getting somewhere near the center of the earth. Let me see: that would be four thousand miles down, I think—yes, that's about the right distance—but then I wonder what Latitude or Longitude I've got to?" (Alice had not the slightest idea what Latitude was, or Longitude either, but she thought they were nice grand words to say.)

Presently she began again. "I wonder if I shall fall right through the earth! How funny it'll seem to come out among the people that walk with their heads downwards!—But I shall have to ask them what the name of the country is, you know. Please, ma'am, is this New Zealand? Or Australia? And what an ignorant little girl she'll think me for asking! No, it'll never do to ask: perhaps I shall see it written up somewhere."

Down, down, down. There was nothing else to do, so Alice soon began talking again. "Dinah'll miss me very much tonight, I should think!" (Dinah was the cat.) "I hope they'll remember her saucer of milk at tea-time. Dinah, my dear! I wish you were down here with me! There are no mice in the air, I'm afraid, but you might catch a bat, and that's very like a mouse, you know. But do cats eat bats, I wonder?" when suddenly, thump! thump! down she came upon a heap of sticks and dry leaves, and the fall was over.

Alice was not a bit hurt, and she jumped up on to her feet in a moment: she looked up, but it was all dark overhead: before her was another long passage, and the White Rabbit was still in sight, hurrying down it.

There was not a moment to be lost: away went Alice like the wind, and was just in time to hear it say, as it turned a corner, "Oh my ears and whiskers, how late it's getting!" She was close behind it when she turned the corner, but the Rabbit was no longer to be seen: she found herself in a long, low hall, which was lit up by a row of lamps hanging from the roof.

There were doors all around the hall, but they were all locked; and when Alice had been all the way down one side and up the other, trying every door, she walked sadly down the middle, wondering how she was ever to get out again.

Suddenly she came upon a little three-legged table, all made of solid glass: there was nothing on it but a tiny golden key, and Alice's first idea was that this might belong to one of the doors of the hall; but, alas! either the locks were too large, or the key was too small, but at any rate it would not open any of them. However, on the second time round, she came upon a low curtain she had not noticed before, and behind it was a little door about fifteen inches high: she tried the little golden key in the lock, and to her great delight it fitted!

Alice opened the door and found that it led into a small passage, not much larger than a rat-hole: she knelt down and looked along the passage into the loveliest garden you ever saw. How she longed to get out of that dark hall, and wander about among those beds of bright flowers and those cool fountains, but she could not even get her head through the doorway; "and even if my head *would* go through," thought poor Alice, "it would be of very little use without my shoulders. Oh, how I wish I could shut up like a telescope! I think I could, if I only knew how to begin." For, you see, so many out-of-the-way things had happened lately, that

Alice had begun to think that very few things indeed were really impossible.

There seemed to be no use in waiting by the little door, so she went back to the table, half hoping she might find another key on it, or at any rate a book of rules for shutting people up like telescopes: this time she found a little bottle on it ("which certainly was not here before," said Alice), and tied around the neck of the bottle was a paper label, with the words "DRINK ME" beautifully printed on it in large letters.

Tied around the neck of the bottle was a paper label,
with the words "DRINK ME" beautifully printed on it in large letters.

It was all very well to say "Drink me," but the wise little Alice was not going to do *that* in a hurry. "No, I'll look first," she said, "and see whether it's marked 'poison' or not"; for she had read several nice little stories about children who had got burnt, and eaten up by wild beasts, and other unpleasant things, all because they *would* not remember the simple rules their friends had taught them.

However, this bottle was *not* marked "poison," so Alice ventured to taste it, and, finding it very nice (it had, in fact, a sort of mixed flavor of cherry-tart, custard, pineapple, roast turkey, toffee, and hot buttered toast), she very soon finished it off.

"What a curious feeling!" said Alice. "I must be shutting up like a telescope!"

And so it was indeed: she was now only ten inches high, and her face brightened up at the thought that she was now the right size for going through the little door into that lovely garden. First, however, she waited for a few minutes to see if she was going to shrink any further: she felt a little nervous about this; "for it might end, you know," said Alice to herself, "in my going out altogether, like a candle. I wonder what I should be like then?" And she tried to fancy what the flame of a candle looks like after the candle is blown out, for she could not remember ever having seen such a thing.

After a while, finding that nothing more happened, she decided on going into the garden at once; but, alas for poor Alice! When she got to the door, she found she had forgotten the little golden key, and when she went back to the table for it, she found she could not possibly reach it: she could see it quite plainly through the glass, and she tried her best to climb up one of the legs of the table, but it was too slippery; and when she had tired herself out with trying, the poor little thing sat down and cried.

"Come, there's no use in crying like that!" said Alice to herself rather sharply. "I advise you to leave off this minute."

Soon her eye fell on a little glass box that was lying under the table; she opened it, and found in it a very small cake, on which the words "EAT ME" were beautifully marked in currants. "Well, I'll eat it," said Alice, "and if it makes me grow larger, I can reach the key; and if it makes me grow smaller, I can creep under the door: so either way I'll get into the garden, and I don't care which happens!"

She ate a little bit, and said anxiously to herself "Which way? Which way?" holding her hand on the top of her head to feel which way it was growing; and she was quite surprised to find that she remained the same size. To be sure, this is what generally happens when one eats cake; but Alice had got so much into the way of expecting nothing but out-of-the-way things to happen, that it seemed quite dull and stupid for life to go on in the common way.

So she set to work, and very soon finished off the cake.

"Curiouser and curiouser!" cried Alice. "Now, I'm opening out like the largest telescope that ever was! Goodbye, feet!" (for when she looked down at her feet, they seemed to be almost out of sight, they were getting so far off). Just at this moment her head struck once against the roof of the hall: in fact she was now rather more than nine feet high, and she at once took up the little golden key and hurried off to the garden door.

Poor Alice! It was as much as she could do, lying down on one side, to look through into the garden with one eye; but to get through was more hopeless than ever: she sat down and began to cry again.

"You ought to be ashamed of yourself," said Alice, "a

great girl like you to go on crying in this way! Stop this moment, I tell you!" But she went on all the same, shedding gallons of tears, until there was a large pool around her, about four inches deep, and reaching half down the hall.

After a time she heard a little pattering of feet in the distance, and she hastily dried her eyes to see what was coming. It was the White Rabbit returning splendidly dressed, with a pair of white kid-gloves in one hand and a large fan in the other: he came trotting along in a great hurry, muttering to himself, as he came, "Oh! The Duchess, the Duchess! Oh! *Won't* she be savage if I've kept her waiting!" Alice felt so desperate that she was ready to ask help of anyone: so, when the Rabbit came near her, she began, in a low, timid voice, "If you please, Sir—" The Rabbit was startled, and dropped the white kid-gloves and the fan, and scurried away into the darkness as hard as he could go.

Alice took up the fan and gloves and, as the hall was very hot, she kept fanning herself all the time she went on talking. "Dear, dear! How odd everything is today! And yesterday things went on just as usual, I wonder if I've changed in the night? Let me think: *was* I the same when I got up this morning? I almost think I can remember feeling a little different. But if I'm not the same, the next question is 'Who in the world am I?' Ah, *that's* the great puzzle!" And she began thinking over all the children she knew that were of the same age as herself, to see if she could have been changed for any of them.

"I'll try if I know all the things I used to know. I'll try and say '*How doth the little—*,'" and she crossed her hands on her lap as if she were saying lessons, and began to repeat it, but her voice sounded strange, and the words did not come the same as they used to do:

The Rabbit was startled, and dropped the white-kid gloves
and the fan, and scurried away.

"How doth the little crocodile
Improve his shining tail,
And pour the waters of the Nile
On every golden scale!

How cheerfully he seems to grin,
How neatly spreads his claws,
And welcomes little fishes in
With gently smiling jaws!"

"I'm sure those are not the right words," said poor Alice, and her eyes filled with tears again as she went on, "I'll stay down here till I'm somebody else—but, oh dear!" cried Alice, with a sudden burst of tears, "I am so *very* tired of being all alone here!"

As she said this she looked down at her hands, and was surprised to see that she had put on one of the Rabbit's little white kid-gloves while she was talking. "How can I have done that?" she thought. "I must be growing small again." She got up and went to the table to measure herself by it, and found that she was now about two feet high, and was going on shrinking rapidly: she soon found out that the cause of this was the fan she was holding, and she dropped it hastily, just in time to save herself from shrinking away altogether.

"That was a narrow escape!" said Alice, a good deal frightened at the sudden change. "And now for the garden!" And she ran with all speed back to the little door; but, alas! the little door was shut again, and the little golden key was lying on the glass table as before, "and things are worse than ever," thought the poor child, "for I never was so small as this before, never!"

As she said these words her foot slipped, and in another moment, splash! she was up to her chin in salt-water. Her first idea was that she had somehow fallen into the sea. However, she soon made out that she was in the pool of tears which she had wept when she was nine feet high.

"I wish I hadn't cried so much!" said Alice, as she swam about. "I shall be punished for it now, I suppose, by being drowned in my own tears!"

Just then she heard something splashing about in the pool a little way off, and she swam nearer to make out what it was: at first she thought it must be a walrus or hippopotamus, but then she remembered how small she was now, and she soon made out that it was only a mouse that had slipped in like herself.

"O Mouse, do you know the way out of this pool? I am very tired of swimming about here, O Mouse!" (Alice thought this must be the right way of speaking to a mouse; she had never done such a thing before.) The mouse looked at her, and seemed to wink with one of its little eyes, but it said nothing.

"Perhaps it doesn't understand English," thought Alice. "I daresay it's a French mouse." So she began again: "Où est ma chatte?" which was the first sentence in her French lesson-book. (It means, "Where is my cat?") The Mouse gave a sudden leap out of the water, and seemed to quiver all over with fright. "Oh, I beg your pardon!" cried Alice, afraid that she had hurt the poor animal's feelings. "I quite forgot you didn't like cats."

"Not like cats!" cried the Mouse. "Would *you* like cats, if you were me?"

"Well, perhaps not," said Alice. "But don't be angry about it. And yet I wish I could show you our cat Dinah. I think you'd take a fancy to cats, if you could only see her. She is such a dear quiet thing." Alice went on, as she swam lazily about in the pool, "Dinah sits purring so nicely by the fire, licking her paws and washing her face—and she is such a nice soft thing to pet—and she's such a capital one for catching mice—oh, I beg your pardon!" cried Alice again, for this time the Mouse was bristling all over, and she felt certain it must be really offended. "We won't talk about her any more if you'd rather not."

"We, indeed!" cried the Mouse, who was trembling down to the end of his tail. "As if I would talk on such a subject! Our family always *hated* cats: nasty, low, vulgar things! Don't let me hear the name again!"

"I won't, indeed!" said Alice, in a great hurry to change the subject of conversation. "Are you—are you fond—of—of dogs?" The Mouse did not answer, so Alice went on eagerly: "There is such a nice little dog, near our house, I should like to show you! A little bright-eyed terrier, you know, with oh, such long curly brown hair! And it'll fetch things when you throw them, and it'll sit up and beg for its dinner, and all sorts of things—I can't remember half of them—and it belongs to a farmer, you know, and he says it's so useful, it's worth a hundred pounds! He says it kills the rats and—oh dear!" cried Alice in a sorrowful tone. "I'm afraid I've offended it again!" For the Mouse was swimming away from her as hard as it could go, and making quite a commotion in the pool as it went.

So she called softly after it, "Mouse dear! Do come back again, and we won't talk about cats, or dogs either, if you don't like them!" When the Mouse heard this, it turned round and swam slowly back to her; its face was quite pale, and it said, "Let us get to the shore, and then I'll tell you my history, and you'll understand why it is I hate cats and dogs."

It was high time to go, for the pool was getting quite crowded with the birds and animals that had fallen into it: there was a Duck and a Dodo,* a Lory† and an Eaglet, and several other curious creatures. Alice led the way, and the whole party swam to the shore.

They were indeed an odd-looking party that assembled on the bank—the birds with draggled feathers, the animals with their fur clinging close to them, and all dripping wet, cross, and uncomfortable.

The first question was how to get dry again.

"I suggest," said the Dodo, "that we take up the immediate adoption of energetic remedies—"

"Speak English!" said the Eaglet. "I don't know the meaning of half those long words, and, what's more, I don't believe you do either!"

"What I was going to say," said the Dodo in an offended tone, "was, that the best thing to get us dry would be a Caucus-race."

"What is a Caucus-race?" asked Alice.

"Why," said the Dodo, "the best way to explain it is to do it." (And, as you might like to try the thing yourself some winter-day, I will tell you how the Dodo managed it.)

First it marked out a race-course, in a sort of circle ("The exact shape doesn't matter," it said), and then all the party were placed along the course, here and there. There was no "One, two, three, and away!" but they began running when they liked, and left off when they liked, so that it was not easy to know when the race was over. However, when they had been running half an hour or so, and were quite dry again, the Dodo suddenly called out, "The race is over!" and they all crowded round it, panting, and asked, "But who has won?"

---

*A Dodo is an extinct, heavy, flightless bird.
†A Lory is an Australian parrot.

This question the Dodo could not answer without a great deal of thought, and it stood for a long time with one finger pressed to its forehead, while the rest waited in silence. At last the Dodo said, "*Everybody* has won, and *all* must have prizes."

"But who is to give the prizes?" a chorus of voices asked.

"Why, *she,* of course," said the Dodo, pointing to Alice; and the whole party at once crowded round her, calling out, "Prizes! Prizes!"

Alice had no idea what to do, and in despair put her hand in her pocket, and pulled out a box of candy, and handed them round as prizes. There was exactly one apiece, all round.

"But she must have a prize herself, you know," said the Mouse.

"Of course," the Dodo replied. "What else have you got in your pocket?" it went on, turning to Alice.

"Only a thimble," said Alice.

"Hand it over here," said the Dodo.

Then they all crowded round her once more, while the Dodo presented the thimble, saying, "We beg your acceptance of this elegant thimble." When it had finished this short speech, they all cheered.

Alice thought the whole thing very silly, but she did not dare laugh; and, as she could not think of anything to say, she bowed, and took the thimble.

They sat down again in a ring, and begged the Mouse to tell them something.

"You promised to tell me your history, you know," said Alice, "and why it is you hate—C and D," she added in a whisper.

"Mine is a long and sad tale!" said the Mouse, turning to Alice, and sighing.

"It is a long tail, certainly," said Alice, looking down

"Hand it over here," said the Dodo.

with wonder at the Mouse's tail; "but why do you call it sad?"

"You insult me by talking such nonsense!" said the Mouse, getting up and walking away.

"But you're so easily offended, you know!"

The Mouse only growled in reply.

"Please come back and finish your story!" Alice called after it. And the others all joined in chorus, "Yes, please do!" But the Mouse only shook its head impatiently, and walked a little quicker.

"What a pity it wouldn't stay!" sighed the Lory, as soon as it was quite out of sight.

"I wish I had our Dinah here, I know I do!" said Alice aloud, addressing nobody in particular. "*She'd* soon fetch it back!"

"And who is Dinah, if I might venture to ask the question?" said the Lory.

Alice replied eagerly, for she was always ready to talk about her pet: "Dinah's our cat. And she's such a capital one for catching mice! And oh, I wish you could see her after the birds! Why, she'll eat a little bird as soon as look at it!"

This speech caused a remarkable sensation among the party. With various excuses, they all moved off, and Alice was left alone.

"I wish I hadn't mentioned Dinah!" she said to herself. "Nobody seems to like her, down here, and I'm sure she's the best cat in the world! Oh, my dear Dinah! I wonder if I shall ever see you any more!" And here poor Alice began to cry again, for she felt very lonely. In a little while, however, she again heard a little pattering of footsteps in the distance, and she looked up eagerly, half hoping that the Mouse had changed his mind, and was coming back to finish his story.

2. The Rabbit Sends in a Little Bill

It was the White Rabbit, trotting slowly back again, and looking anxiously about as it went, as if it had lost something; and she heard it muttering to itself, "The Duchess! The Duchess! Oh my dear paws! Oh my fur and whiskers! She'll have me killed, as sure as ferrets are ferrets! Where *can* I have dropped them, I wonder?" Alice guessed in a moment that it was looking for the fan and the pair of white kid-gloves, and she very good-naturedly began hunting about for them, but they were nowhere to be seen—everything seemed to have changed since her swim in the pool; and the great hall, with the glass table and the little door, had vanished completely.

Very soon the Rabbit noticed Alice, as she went hunting about, and called out to her, "Why, Mary Ann, what *are* you doing here? Run home this moment, and fetch me a pair of gloves and a fan! Quick, now!" And Alice was so frightened that she ran off at once in the direction it pointed to, without trying to explain the mistake that it had made.

"He took me for his housemaid," she said to herself as she ran. "How surprised he'll be when he finds out who I am! But I'd better take him his fan and gloves—that is, if I can find them." As she said this, she came upon a neat little house, on the door of which was a bright brass plate with the name "W. RABBIT" engraved upon it. She went in without knocking, and hurried upstairs, in great fear that she should meet the real

Mary Ann, and be sent out of the house before she had found the fan and gloves.

"How strange it seems," Alice said to herself, "to be doing errands for a rabbit! I suppose Dinah'll be sending me on errands next!" She now found her way into a tidy little room with a table in the window, and on it (as she had hoped) a fan and two or three pairs of tiny white kid-gloves: she took up the fan and a pair of gloves, and was just going to leave the room, when her eye fell upon a little bottle that stood near the looking-glass. There was no label this time with the words "DRINK ME," but nevertheless she uncorked it and put it to her lips. "I know something interesting is sure to happen," she said to herself, "whenever I eat or drink anything: so I'll just see what this bottle does. I do hope it'll make me grow large again, for really I'm quite tired of being such a tiny little thing!"

It did so indeed, and much sooner than she had expected: before she had drunk half the bottle, she found her head pressing against the ceiling, and had to stoop to save her neck from being broken. She hastily put down the bottle, saying to herself, "That's quite enough—I hope I shan't grow any more. As it is, I can't get out the door.—I do wish I hadn't drunk quite so much!"

Alas! It was too late to wish that! She went on growing, and growing, and very soon had to kneel down on the floor: in another minute there was not even room for this, and she tried the effect of lying down with one elbow against the door, and the other arm curled round her head. Still she went on growing, and, in a desperate hope, she put one arm out of the window, and one foot up the chimney, and said to herself, "Now I can do no more, whatever happens."

Luckily for Alice, the little magic bottle had now had

Still she went on growing, and, in a desperate hope,
she put one arm out of the window, and one foot up the chimney.

its full effect, and she grew no larger: still it was very
uncomfortable, and, as there seemed to be no sort of
chance of her ever getting out of the room again, no
wonder she felt unhappy.

"It was much pleasanter at home," thought poor
Alice, "when one wasn't always growing larger and
smaller, and being ordered about by mice and rabbits.
I almost wish I hadn't gone down that rabbit-hole—and
yet—and yet—it's rather curious, you know, this sort of
life! I do wonder what *can* have happened to me! When
I used to read fairy tales, I fancied that kind of thing
never happened, and now here I am in the middle of
one! There ought to be a book written about me, that
there ought! And when I grow up, I'll write it."

She now heard a voice outside and stopped to listen. "Mary Ann! Mary Ann!" said the voice. "Fetch me my gloves this moment!" Then came a little pattering of feet on the stairs. Alice knew it was the Rabbit coming to look for her, and she trembled till she shook the house, quite forgetting that she was now about a thousand times as large as the Rabbit, and had no reason to be afraid of it.

Presently the Rabbit came up to the door, and tried to open it; but, as the door opened inwards, and Alice's elbow was pressed hard against it, that attempt proved a failure. Alice heard it say to itself, "Then I'll go round and get in at the window."

"That you won't!" thought Alice, and, after waiting till she fancied she heard the Rabbit just under the window, she suddenly spread out her hand, and made a snatch in the air. She did not get hold of anything, but she heard a little shriek and a fall, and a crash of broken glass, from which she concluded that it was just possible it had fallen into a cucumber-frame, or something of that sort.

Next came an angry voice—the Rabbit's—"Pat! Pat! Where are you?" And then a voice she had never heard before, "Sure then I'm here!"

"Come help me out of this!" (Sounds of more broken glass.) "Now tell me, Pat, what's that in the window?"

"Sure, it's an arm, yer honor!"

"An arm, you goose! Who ever saw one that size? Why, it fills the whole window!"

"Sure it does, yer honor: but it's an arm for all that."

"Well, it's got no business there: go and take it away!"

There was a long silence after this, and Alice could only hear whispers now and then; such as "Sure, I don't like it, yer honor, at all, at all!" "Do as I tell you, you coward!" and at last she spread out her hand again, and made another snatch in the air. This time there were *two* little shrieks, and more sounds of broken glass. "What a number of cucumber-frames there must be!" thought Alice. "I wonder what they'll do next! As for pulling me out of the window, I only wish they *could!* I'm sure I don't want to stay in here any longer!"

She waited for some time without hearing anything more: at last came a rumbling of little cart-wheels, and the sounds of a good many voices all talking together: she made out the words: "Where's the other ladder?— Why, I didn't bring but one. Bill's got the other.—Bill! Fetch it here, lad!—Here, put 'em up in this corner.— Here, Bill! Catch hold of this rope.—Will the roof bear it?—Mind that loose slate.—Who's to go down the chimney?—Nay, I shan't! *You* do it!—*That* I won't, then!—Bill's got to go down.—Here, Bill! The master says you've got to go down the chimney!"

"Oh! So Bill's got to come down the chimney, has he?" said Alice to herself. "Why, they seem to put everything upon Bill. I wouldn't be in Bill's shoes for a good deal; this fireplace is narrow, to be sure; but I *think* I can kick a little!"

She drew her foot as far down the chimney as she could, and waited till she heard a little animal (she couldn't guess of what sort it was) scratching and scrambling about in the chimney above her: then, say-ing to herself, "This is Bill," she gave one sharp kick, and waited to see what would happen next.

The first thing she heard was a general chorus of, "There goes Bill!" then the Rabbit's voice alone— "Catch him, you by the hedge!" then silence, and then another confusion of voices—"Hold up his head.— Medicine now.—Don't choke him.—How was it, old fel-low? What happened to you?"

Last came a little feeble, squeaking voice. ("That's

Bill," thought Alice.) "Well, I hardly know.—No more, thank ye; I'm better now.—All I know is, something comes at me like a Jack-in-the-box, and up I goes like a skyrocket!"

"So you did, old fellow!" said the others.

"We must burn the house down!" said the Rabbit's voice. And Alice called out, as loud as she could, "If you do, I'll set Dinah at you!"

There was a dead silence instantly, and Alice thought to herself, "If they had any sense, they'd take the roof off!"

After a minute or two they began moving about again, and Alice heard the Rabbit say, "A barrowful will do, to begin with."

"A barrowful of *what*?" thought Alice. But she had not long to doubt, for the next moment a shower of little pebbles came rattling in at the window, and some of them hit her in the face. "I'll put a stop to this," she said to herself, and shouted out, "You'd better not do that again!" which produced another dead silence.

Alice noticed, with some surprise, that the pebbles were all turning into little cakes as they lay on the floor, and a bright idea came into her head. "If I eat one of these cakes," she thought, "it's sure to make *some* change in my size; and, as it can't possibly make me larger, it must make me smaller, I suppose."

So she swallowed one of the cakes, and was delighted to find that she began shrinking. As soon as she was small enough to get through the door, she ran out of the house, and found quite a crowd of little animals and birds waiting outside. The poor little Lizard, Bill, was in the middle, being held up by two guinea-pigs, who were giving it something out of a bottle. They all made a rush at Alice the moment she appeared; but she ran off as hard as she could, and soon found herself safe in a thick wood.

"The first thing I've got to do," said Alice to herself, as she wandered about in the wood, "is to grow to my right size again; and the second thing is to find my way into that lovely garden. I think that will be the best plan."

It sounded like an excellent plan, no doubt: the only difficulty was, that she had not the smallest idea how to set about it. "Let me see—how *is* it to be managed? I suppose I ought to eat or drink something or other; but the great question is 'What?'"

Alice looked all round her at the flowers and the blades of grass, but she could not see anything that looked like the right thing to eat or drink under the circumstances. There was a large mushroom growing near her, about the same height as herself; and, when she had looked under it, and on both sides of it, and behind it, it occurred to her that she might as well look and see what was on top of it.

She stretched herself up on tiptoe, and peeped over the edge of the mushroom, and her eyes immediately met those of a large blue caterpillar that was sitting on the top, with its arms folded, quietly smoking a long pipe, and taking not the smallest notice of her or of anything else.

The Caterpillar and Alice looked at each other for some time in silence: at last the Caterpillar took the pipe out of its mouth, and addressed her in a sleepy voice: "Who are *you*?"

Alice replied, rather shyly, "I—I hardly know, Sir, just at present—at least I know who I *was* when I got up this morning, but I think I must have been changed several times since then."

*Her eyes immediately met those of a large blue caterpillar
that was sitting on the top.*

"What do you mean by that?" said the Caterpillar. "Explain yourself!"

"I can't explain *myself*, I'm afraid, Sir," said Alice, "because I'm not myself, you see."

"I don't see," said the Caterpillar.

"I'm afraid I can't put it more clearly," Alice replied, very politely, "for I can't understand it myself, to begin with; and being so many different sizes in a day is very confusing."

"It isn't," said the Caterpillar.

"Well, perhaps you haven't found it so yet," said Alice; "but when you have to turn into a chrysalis—you will some day, you know—and then after that into a butterfly, I should think you'll feel it a little odd, won't you?"

"Not a bit," said the Caterpillar.

"Well, perhaps *your* feelings may be different," said Alice. "All I know is, it would feel very odd to *me*."

"You!" said the Caterpillar. "Who are *you*?"

Which brought them back to the beginning of the conversation.

Alice replied, "I think you ought to tell me who *you* are, first."

"Why?" said the Caterpillar.

Here was another puzzling question; and, as Alice could not think of any good reason, and the Caterpillar seemed to be in a *very* unpleasant state of mind, she turned away.

"Come back!" the Caterpillar called after her. "I've something important to say!"

Alice turned and came back.

"Keep your temper," said the Caterpillar.

"Is that all?"

"No," said the Caterpillar.

Alice thought she might as well wait for his next

words, as she had nothing else to do, and perhaps after all it might tell her something worth hearing. For some minutes it puffed away on its pipe without speaking; but at last it unfolded its arms, took the pipe out of its mouth again, and said, "So you think you've changed, do you?"

"I'm afraid I have, Sir," said Alice. "I can't remember things as I used to—and I don't keep the same size for ten minutes together!"

"What size do you want to be?" said the Caterpillar.

"Well, I should like to be a little larger, Sir, if you wouldn't mind," said Alice. "Three inches is such a poor height to be."

"It is a very good height indeed!" said the Caterpillar angrily (it was exactly three inches high).

"But I'm not used to it!" said Alice.

"You'll get used to it in time," said the Caterpillar; and it put the pipe into its mouth, and began smoking again. In a minute or two it took the pipe out of its mouth, and yawned once or twice. Then it got down off the mushroom, and crawled away into the grass, remarking as it went, "One side will make you grow taller, and the other side will make you grow shorter."

"One side of *what*? The other side of *what*?" thought Alice to herself.

"Of the mushroom," said the Caterpillar, just as if she had asked it aloud; and in another moment it was out of sight.

Alice remained looking at the mushroom for a minute, trying to make out which were the two sides of it; and, as it was perfectly round, she found this a very difficult question. However, at last she stretched her arms round it as far as they would go, and broke off a bit of the edge with each hand.

"And now which is which?" she said to herself, and

nibbled a little of the right-hand bit to try the effect. The next moment she felt a blow underneath her chin: it had struck her foot!

She was a good deal frightened by this very sudden change, but she felt that there was no time to be lost, as she was shrinking rapidly: so she set to work at once to eat some of the other bit. Her chin was pressed so closely against her foot, that there was hardly room to open her mouth; but she did at last, and managed to swallow a morsel of the left-hand bit.

"Come, my head's free at last!" said Alice in a tone of delight, which changed into alarm in another moment, when she found that her shoulders were nowhere to be found: all she could see, when she looked down, was an immense length of neck, which seemed to rise like a stalk out of a sea of green leaves that lay far below her.

"What *can* all that green stuff be?" said Alice. "And where have my shoulders got to? And oh, my poor hands, how is it I can't see you?" She was moving them about, as she spoke, but no result seemed to follow, except a little shaking among the distant green leaves.

As there seemed to be no chance of getting her hands up to her head, she tried to get her head down to *them,* and was delighted to find that her neck would bend easily in any direction, like a serpent. She had just succeeded in curving it down into a graceful zigzag, and was going to dive in among the leaves, which she found to be nothing but the tops of the trees under which she had been wandering.

Alice crouched down among the trees as well as she could, for her neck kept getting entangled among the branches, and every now and then she had to stop and untwist it. After a while she remembered that she still held the pieces of mushroom in her hands, and she set to work very carefully, nibbling first at one and then at

the other, and growing sometimes taller, and sometimes shorter, until she had succeeded in bringing herself down to her usual height.

It was so long since she had been anything near the
right size, that it felt quite strange at first; but she got
used to it in a few minutes, and began talking to herself,
as usual. "Come, there's half my plan done now! How
puzzling all these changes are! I'm never sure what I'm
going to be, from one minute to another! However, I've
got back to my right size: the next thing is, to get into
that beautiful garden—how *is* that to be done, I wonder?" As she said this, she came suddenly upon an
open place, with a little house in it about four feet high.
"Whoever lives there," thought Alice, "it'll never do to
come upon them *this* size: why, I should frighten them
out of their wits!" So she began nibbling at the right-
hand bit again, and did not venture to go near the
house till she had brought herself down to nine inches
high.

3. Pig and Pepper

For a minute or two she stood looking at the house, and wondering what to do next, when suddenly a footman in his uniform came running out of the wood—(she considered him to be a footman because he was in uniform: otherwise, judging by his face only, she would have called him a fish)—and rapped loudly at the door with his knuckles. It was opened by another footman in uniform, with a round face, and large eyes like a frog; and both footmen, Alice noticed, had powdered hair that curled all over their heads. She felt very curious to know what it was all about, and crept a little way out of the wood to listen.

The Fish-Footman began by producing from under his arm a great letter, nearly as large as himself, and this he handed over to the other, saying, in a solemn tone, "For the Duchess. An invitation from the Queen to play croquet." The Frog-Footman repeated, in the same solemn tone, only changing the order of the words a little, "From the Queen. An invitation for the Duchess to play croquet."

Then they both bowed, and the Fish-Footman left, and the other sat sitting on the ground near the door, staring up at the sky.

Alice went timidly up to the door, and knocked.

"There's no sort of use in knocking," said the Footman, "and that for two reasons. First, because I'm on the same side of the door as you are; secondly, because they're making such a noise inside, no one

29

*The Fish-Footman began by producing from under his arm
a great letter, nearly as large as himself.*

could possibly hear you." And certainly there *was* a
most extraordinary noise going on within—a constant
howling and sneezing, and every now and then a great
crash, as if a dish had been broken to pieces.

"Please, then," said Alice, "how am I to get in?"

At this moment the door of the house opened, and a
large plate came skimming out, straight at the
Footman's head; it just missed his nose, and broke to
pieces against one of the trees behind him.

"Are you to get in at all?" said the Footman, exactly
as if nothing had happened. "That's the first question,
you know."

"But what am I to do?" said Alice.

"Anything you like," said the Footman, and began
whistling.

So she opened the door and went in, right into a large kitchen, which was full of smoke from one end to the other: the Duchess was sitting on a three-legged stool in the middle, nursing a baby: the cook was leaning over the fire, stirring a large cauldron which seemed to be full of soup.

"There's certainly too much pepper in that soup!" Alice said to herself, as well as she could for sneezing.

There was certainly too much of it in the *air*. Even the Duchess sneezed occasionally; and as for the baby, it was sneezing and howling alternately without a moment's pause. The only two creatures in the kitchen that did *not* sneeze were the cook, and a large cat, which was lying on the hearth and grinning from ear to ear.

"Please would you tell me," said Alice, a little timidly, "why your cat grins like that?"

"It's a Cheshire-Cat," said the Duchess, "and that's why, Pig!"

She said the last word with such heat that Alice quite jumped; but she saw in another moment that it was addressed to the baby, and not to her, so she took courage and went on again: "I didn't know that Cheshire-Cats always grinned; in fact, I didn't know that cats *could* grin."

"They all can," said the Duchess; "and most of 'em do."

"I don't know of any that do," Alice said very politely.

"You don't know much," said the Duchess; "and that's a fact."

Alice did not at all like the tone of this remark, and thought it would be well to introduce some other subject of conversation. While she was trying to fix on one, the cook took the cauldron of soup off the fire, and at once set to work throwing everything within her reach at the Duchess and the baby—the fire-irons came first; then followed a shower of sauce-pans, plates, and dishes. The Duchess took no notice of them even when they hit her; and the baby was howling so much already, that it was quite impossible to say whether the blows hurt it or not.

"Oh, please mind what you're doing!" cried Alice, jumping up and down in an agony of terror. "Oh, there goes his precious nose!" as a large saucepan flew close by it, and very nearly carried it off.

"If everybody minded their own business," the Duchess said, in a hoarse growl, "the world would go round a deal faster than it does."

"Which would *not* be an advantage," said Alice. "Just think what work it would make with the day and night! You see the earth takes twenty-four hours to turn round on its axis—"

"Talking of axes," said the Duchess, "chop off her head!"

Alice glanced at the cook, to see if she meant to take the hint; but the cook was busily stirring the soup, and seemed not to be listening, so she went on again: "Twenty-four hours, I *think*; or it is twelve? I—"

"Oh, don't bother *me*!" said the Duchess. "I never could stand numbers!" And with that she began nursing her child again, singing a sort of lullaby as she did so.

When the song was over, the Duchess said to Alice, "Here! You may hold it a bit, if you like!" And the woman flung the baby at Alice. "I must go and get ready to play croquet with the Queen," and she hurried out of the room. The cook threw a frying-pan after her as she went, but it just missed her.

Alice caught the baby, but it was a strangely shaped little creature, and held out its arms and legs in all directions, "just like a starfish," thought Alice. The poor little thing was snorting like a steam-engine when she caught it, and kept doubling itself up and straightening itself out again, so that altogether, for the first minute or two, it was as much as she could do to hold it.

As soon as she had made out the proper way of holding it, she carried it out into the open air. The baby grunted, and Alice looked very anxiously into its face to see what was the matter with it. There could be no doubt that it had a *very* upturned nose, much more like a snout than a real nose: also its eyes were getting extremely small for a baby: altogether Alice did not like the look of the thing at all. "But perhaps it was only sobbing," she thought, and looked into its eyes again, to see if there were any tears.

No, there were no tears. "If you're going to turn into a pig, my dear," said Alice, "I'll have nothing more to do

"If you're going to turn into a pig, my dear," said Alice, "I'll have nothing more to do with you."

with you. Mind now!" The poor little thing sobbed again (or grunted, it was impossible to say which), and they went on for some while in silence.

Alice was just beginning to think to herself, "Now, what am I to do with this creature, when I get it home?" when it grunted again, so violently, that she looked down into its face in some alarm. This time there could be *no* mistake about it: it was a pig, and she felt that it would be quite absurd for her to carry it any further.

So she set the little creature down, and felt quite relieved to see it trot away into the wood. "If it had grown up," she said to herself, "it would have made an ugly child: but it makes rather a handsome pig, I think." And she began thinking over other children she knew, who might do very well as pigs, when she was a little startled by seeing the Cheshire-Cat sitting on a bough of a tree a few yards off.

The Cat only grinned when it saw Alice. It looked good-natured, she thought: still it had *very* long claws and a great many teeth, so she felt that it ought to be treated with respect.

"Cheshire-Puss," she began, and it grinned a little wider, "would you tell me, please, which way I ought to go from here?"

"That depends a good deal on where you want to get to," said the Cat.

"I don't much care where—" said Alice.

"Then it doesn't matter which way you go," said the Cat.

"—so long as I get *somewhere,*" Alice added.

"Oh, you're sure to do that," said the Cat, "if you only walk long enough."

Alice felt that this could not be denied, so she tried another question. "What sort of people live about here?"

*She was a little startled by seeing the Cheshire-Cat
sitting on a bough of a tree a few yards off.*

"In *that* direction," the Cat said, waving its right paw round, "lives a Hatter: and in *that* direction," waving the other paw, "lives a March Hare. Visit either you like: the're both mad."

"But I don't want to go among mad people," Alice remarked.

"Oh, you can't help that," said the Cat: "we're all mad here. I'm mad. You're mad."

"How do you know I'm mad?" said Alice.

"You must be," said the Cat, "or you wouldn't have come here."

Alice didn't think that proved it at all: however, she went on: "And how do you know that you're mad?"

"To begin with," said the Cat, "a dog's not mad. You grant that?"

"I suppose so."

"Well, then," the Cat went on, "you see a dog growls when it's angry, and wags its tail when it's pleased. Now I growl when I'm pleased, and wag my tail when I'm angry. Therefore I'm mad."

"I call it purring, not growling."

"Call it what you like," said the Cat. "Do you play croquet with the Queen today?"

"I should like to very much," said Alice, "but I haven't been invited yet."

"You'll see me there," said the Cat, and vanished quite slowly, beginning with the end of the tail, and ending with the grin, which remained some time after the rest of it had gone.

"Well! I've often seen a cat without a grin," thought Alice; "but a grin without a cat! It's the most curious thing I ever saw in all my life!"

She had not gone much farther before she came in sight of the house of the March Hare: she thought it must be the right house, because the chimneys were shaped like ears and the roof was thatched with fur. It was so large a house, that she did not like to go nearer till she had nibbled some more of the left-hand bit of mushroom, and raised herself to about two feet high: even then she walked up towards it rather timidly, saying to herself, "Suppose it should be raving mad! I almost wish I'd gone to see the Hatter instead!"

"There's plenty *of room!" said Alice,*
and she sat down in a large armchair at one end of the table.

4. A Mad Tea-Party

There was a table set out under a tree in front of the house, and the March Hare and the Hatter were having tea at it: a Dormouse was sitting between them, fast asleep, and the other two were using it as a cushion, resting their elbows on it, and talking over its head. "Very uncomfortable for the Dormouse," thought Alice; "only as it's asleep, I suppose it doesn't mind."

The table was a large one, but the three were all crowded together at one corner of it. "No room! No room!" they cried out when they saw Alice coming. "There's *plenty* of room!" said Alice, and she sat down in a large armchair at one end of the table.

"Have some wine," the March Hare said.

Alice looked all round the table, but there was nothing on it but tea. "I don't see any wine," she remarked.

"There isn't any," said the March Hare.

"Then it wasn't very polite of you to offer it," said Alice.

"It wasn't very polite of you to sit down without being invited," said the March Hare.

"I didn't know it was *your* table," said Alice: "it's laid for a great many more than three."

The Hatter opened his eyes very wide on hearing this; but all he *said* was, "Why is a raven like a writing-desk?"

"I believe I can guess that," said Alice.

The party sat silent for a minute, while Alice thought over all she could remember about ravens and writing-desks, which wasn't much.

The Hatter was the first to break the silence. "What day of the month is it?" he said, turning to Alice: he had taken his watch out of his pocket, and was looking at it uneasily, shaking it every now and then, and holding it to his ear.

Alice considered a little, and then said, "The fourth."

"Two days wrong!" sighed the Hatter.

Alice had been looking over his shoulder with some curiosity. "What a funny watch!" she remarked. "It tells the day of the month, and doesn't tell what o'clock it is!"

"Why should it?" muttered the Hatter. "Does *your* watch tell you what year it is?"

"Of course not," Alice replied, "but that's because it stays the same year for such a long time together."

"Which is just the case with *mine*," said the Hatter.

Alice felt dreadfully puzzled. The Hatter's remark seemed to her to have no sort of meaning in it, and yet it was certainly English. "I don't quite understand you," she said, as politely as she could.

"Have you guessed the riddle yet?" the Hatter said.

"No, I give up," Alice replied. "What's the answer?"

"I haven't the slightest idea," said the Hatter.

"Nor I," said the March Hare.

"I think you might do something better with the time," Alice said, "than wasting it in asking riddles that have no answers."

"Suppose we change the subject," the March Hare said, yawning. "I vote the young lady tells us a story."

"I'm afraid I don't know one," said Alice.

"Then the Dormouse shall!" cried the Hatter and the Hare. "Wake up, Dormouse!" And they pinched it on both sides at once.

The Dormouse slowly opened its eyes. "I wasn't

asleep," it said. "I heard every word you fellows were saying."

"Tell us a story!" said the March Hare.

"Yes, please do!" pleaded Alice.

"Once upon a time there were three little sisters," the Dormouse began in a great hurry; "and their names were Elsie, Lacie, and Tillie; and they lived at the bottom of a well—"

"What did they live on?" said Alice.

"They lived on molasses," said the Dormouse, after thinking a minute or two.

"They couldn't have done that, you know," Alice gently remarked. "They'd have been ill."

"So they were," said the Dormouse; "*very* ill."

Alice tried a little to imagine what such a strange way of living would be like, but it puzzled her too much: so she went on: "But why did they live at the bottom of a well?"

"Take some more tea," the March Hare said to Alice.

"I've had nothing yet," Alice replied, "so I can't take more." However, she helped herself to some tea and bread-and-butter, and then turned to the Dormouse, and repeated her question. "Why did they live at the bottom of a well?"

The Dormouse again took a minute or two to think about it, and then said, "It was a molasses-well.—And so these three little sisters—they were learning to draw, you know—"

"What did they draw?" said Alice.

"Molasses," said the Dormouse.

"I want a clean cup," interrupted the Hatter. "Let's all move one place over."

He moved on as he spoke, and the Dormouse followed him: the March Hare moved into the Dormouse's place, and Alice rather unwillingly took the place of the March Hare. The Hatter was the only one who got any advantage from the change; and Alice was a good deal worse off than before, as the March Hare had just upset the milk-jug into his plate.

Alice did not wish to offend the Dormouse, but she said, "I don't understand. Where did they draw the molasses from?"

"You can draw water out of a water-well," said the Hatter, "so I should think you could draw molasses out of a molasses-well."

This answer so confused poor Alice that she let the Dormouse go on for some time without interrupting it.

"They were learning to draw," the Dormouse went on, yawning and rubbing its eyes, for it was getting very sleepy; "and they drew all manner of things—everything that begins with an M—"

"Why with an M?" asked Alice.

"Why not?" said the March Hare.

Alice was silent.

The Dormouse closed its eyes by this time, and was going off in a doze; but, on being pinched by the Hatter, it woke up again with a little shriek, and went on: "—that begins with an M, such as mouse-traps, and the moon, and memory, and muchness—you know you say things are 'much of a muchness'—did you ever see such a thing as a drawing of muchness?"

"Really, now you ask me," said Alice, "I don't think—"

"Then you shouldn't talk!" said the Hatter.

This piece of rudeness was more than Alice could bear: she got up in great disgust, and walked off: the Dormouse fell asleep instantly, and neither of the others took the least notice of her going, though she looked back once or twice, half hoping that they would call after her.

"At any rate I'll never go *there* again!" said Alice, as she picked her way through the wood. "It's the stupidest tea-party I ever was at in all my life!"

Just as she said this, she noticed that one of the trees had a door leading right into it. "That's very curious!" she thought. "But everything's curious today. I think I may as well go in at once." And in she went.

Once more she found herself in the long hall, and close to the little glass table. "I'll manage better this time," she said to herself, and began by taking the little golden key, and unlocking the door that led into the garden. Then she set to work nibbling at the mushroom (she had kept a piece of it in her pocket) till she was about a foot high: then she walked down the little passage; and *then*—she found herself at last in the beautiful garden, among the bright flower-beds and the cool fountains.

She noticed that one of the trees had a door leading right into it.

A large rose-tree stood near the entrance of the garden: the roses growing on it were white, but there were three gardeners at it, busily painting them red. Alice thought this a very curious thing, and she went nearer to watch them, and, just as she came up to them, she heard one of them say, "Look out now, Five! Don't go splashing paint over me like that!"

"I couldn't help it," said Five. "Seven knocked my elbow."

On which Seven looked up and said, "That's right, Five! Always lay the blame on others!"

"*You'd* better not talk!" said Five. "I heard the Queen say only yesterday you deserved to be beheaded."

"What for?" said the one who had spoken first.

"That's none of *your* business, Two!" said Seven. Seven's eyes chanced to fall upon Alice, as she stood watching them, and he and others looked round and then bowed low.

"Would you tell me, please," said Alice, "why you are painting these roses?"

Two said, "Why, the fact is, you see, Miss, this here ought to have been a *red* rose tree, and we put a white one in by mistake; and, if the Queen was to find out, we should all have our heads cut off, you know. So you see, Miss, we're doing our best, before she comes, to—" At this moment, Five, who had been looking across the garden, called out, "The Queen! The Queen!" and the three gardeners instantly threw themselves flat upon their faces. There was a sound of many footsteps, and Alice looked round, eager to see the Queen.

First came the ten soldiers carrying clubs: these were all shaped like the three gardeners, long and flat, with their hands and feet at the corners: next the ten courtiers: these were ornamented all over with diamonds, and walked two and two, as the soldiers did.

After these came the royal children: there were ten of them, and the little dears came jumping merrily along, hand in hand, in couples: they were all ornamented with hearts. Next came the guests, mostly Kings and

The roses growing on it were white,
but there were three gardeners at it, busily painting them red.

Queens, and among them Alice recognized the White Rabbit: it went by without noticing her. Then followed the Knave of Hearts, carrying the King's crown on a red velvet cushion; and last of all this grand parade, came THE KING AND QUEEN OF HEARTS.

Alice was rather doubtful whether she ought not to lie down on her face like the three gardeners, but she could not remember ever having heard of such a rule, "and besides, what would be the use of a procession," thought she, "if people had all to lie down on their faces, so that they couldn't see it?" So she stood where she was, and waited.

When the procession came opposite to Alice, they all stopped and looked at her, and the Queen said, "Who is this?" She said it to the Knave of Hearts, who only bowed and smiled in reply.

"Idiot!" said the Queen, tossing her head, and, turning to Alice, she went on: "What's your name, child?"

"My name is Alice, so please your Majesty," said Alice very politely; but she added, to herself, "Why, they're only a pack of cards, after all. I needn't be afraid of them!"

"And who are these?" said the Queen, pointing to the three gardeners who were lying face down round the rose-tree.

"How should *I* know?" said Alice. "It's no business of *mine*."

The Queen turned red with fury, and began screaming, "Off with her head! Off with—"

"Nonsense!" said Alice.

"The King laid his hand upon the Queen's arm, and said, "Consider, my dear: she is only a child!"

The Queen turned angrily away from him, and, pointing to the gardeners, said to the Knave, "Turn them over!"

The Knave did so, very carefully, with one foot.

"Get up!" said the Queen, and three gardeners instantly jumped up, and began bowing to the King, the Queen, the royal children, and everybody else.

"Leave off that!" screamed the Queen. "What have you been doing here?"

"May it please your Majesty," said Two, going down on one knee as he spoke, "we were trying—"

"I see!" said the Queen, who had meanwhile been examining the roses. "Off with their heads!" and the procession moved on, three of the soldiers remaining behind to execute the gardeners, who ran to Alice for protection.

"You shan't be beheaded!" said Alice, and she put them into a large flower-pot that stood near. The three soldiers wandered about for a minute or two, looking for them, and then quietly marched off after the others.

"Are their heads off?" shouted the Queen.

"Their heads are gone, if it please your Majesty!" the soldiers shouted in reply.

"That's right!" shouted the Queen. Turning to Alice, she said, "Can you play croquet?"

"Yes!" replied Alice.

"Come on, then!" roared the Queen.

A few moments later and several yards on, the Queen shouted, "Get to your places!" and people began running about in all directions, tumbling up against each other: however, they got settled down in a minute or two, and the game began.

Alice thought she had never seen such a curious croquet ground in her life: it was all ridges and furrows: the croquet balls were live hedgehogs, and the mallets live flamingoes, and the soldiers had to double themselves up and stand on their hands and feet, to make the arches.

The chief difficulty Alice found at first was in managing her flamingo: she succeeded in getting its body tucked away, comfortably enough, under her arm, with its legs hanging down, but generally, just as she had got

The chief difficulty Alice found at first was in managing her flamingo.

its neck nicely straightened out, and was going to give the hedgehog a blow with its head, it *would* twist itself round and look up in her face, with such a puzzled expression that she could not help bursting out laughing; and when she had got its head down and was going to begin again, it was very provoking to find that the hedgehog had unrolled itself and was crawling away: besides all this, there was generally a ridge or a furrow in the way wherever she wanted to send the hedgehog to, and, as the doubled-up soldiers were always getting up and walking off to other parts of the ground, Alice soon came to find that it was a very difficult game indeed.

The players all played at once, without waiting for turns, quarreling all the while, and fighting for the hedgehogs: and in a very short time the Queen was in a furious passion, and went stamping about, and shouting, "Off with his head!" or "Off with her head!" about once a minute.

Alice began looking about for some way of escape. She noticed a curious appearance in the air: it puzzled her very much at first, but after watching it a minute or two she made it out to be a grin, and she said to herself, "It's the Cheshire-Cat: now I shall have somebody to talk to."

"How are you getting on?" said the Cat, as soon as there was mouth enough for it to speak with.

Alice waited till the eyes appeared, and then nodded. "It's no use speaking to it," she thought, "till its ears have come, or at least one of them." In another minute the whole head appeared, and then Alice put down her flamingo, and began an account of the game, feeling very glad she had someone to listen to her. The Cat seemed to think that there was enough of it now in sight, and no more of it appeared.

"I don't think they play at all fairly," Alice began, "and they all quarrel so dreadfully one can't hear oneself speak—and they don't seem to have any rules in particular: at least, if there are, nobody pays attention to them—and you've no idea how confusing it is all the things being alive."

"How do you like the Queen?" said the Cat in a low voice.

In another minute, the whole head appeared.

"Not at all," said Alice: "she's so extremely—" Just then she noticed that the Queen was close behind her, listening: so she went on, "—likely to win, that it's hardly worth while finishing the game."

The Queen smiled.

"Who *are* you talking to?" said the King, coming up to Alice, and looking at the Cat's head with great curiosity.

"It's a friend of mine—a Cheshire-Cat," said Alice.

"I don't like the look of it at all," said the King.

"It belongs to the Duchess: you'd better ask *her* about it," said Alice.

"She's in prison," said the Queen to the executioner: "fetch her here." And the executioner went off like an arrow.

The Cat's head began fading away the moment the executioner was gone, and, by the time he had come back with the Duchess, it had entirely disappeared: so the King and the executioner ran wildly up and down, looking for it, while the rest of the party went back to the game.

"You can't think how glad I am to see you again, you dear old thing!" said the Duchess, as she tucked her arm into Alice's, and they walked off together.

Alice was very glad to find the Duchess in such a pleasant mood, but she did not much like her keeping so close to her: the Duchess was exactly the right height to rest her chin on Alice's shoulder, and it was an uncomfortably sharp chin. However, she did not like to be rude, so she bore it as well as she could.

"I daresay you're wondering why I don't put my arm round your waist," the Duchess said. "The reason is, that I'm doubtful about the mood of your flamingo. Shall I try anyway?"

"He might bite," Alice replied.

"Very true," said the Duchess: "flamingoes and mustard both bite. And the moral of that is—'Birds of a feather flock together.'"

To Alice's great surprise, the Duchess's voice died away, and the arm that was linked into hers began to tremble. Alice looked up, and there stood the Queen in front of them, with her arms folded, frowning like a thunderstorm.

"A fine day, your Majesty!" the Duchess began in a weak voice.

"Now, I give you fair warning," shouted the Queen, stamping on the ground as she spoke, "either you or your head must be off, and that in about half no time! Take your choice!"

The Duchess took her choice, and was gone in a moment.

"Let's go on with the game," the Queen said to Alice; and Alice was too much frightened to say a word, but slowly followed her back to the croquet ground.

The other guests had taken advantage of the Queen's being gone, and were resting in the shade; however, the moment they saw her, they hurried back to the game, the Queen merely remarking that a moment's delay would cost them their lives.

All the time they were playing the Queen never left off quarreling with the other players and shouting, "Off with his head!" or "Off with her head!" Those whom she sentenced were taken into custody by the soldiers, who of course had to leave off being arches to do this, so that, by the end of half an hour or so, there were no arches left, and all the players, except the King, the Queen, and Alice, were in custody and under sentence of death.

Then the Queen said to Alice, "Have you seen the Mock Turtle* yet?"

"No," said Alice. "I don't even know what a Mock Turtle is."

"It's the thing Mock Turtle Soup is made from," said the Queen. "Come along, then, and he shall tell you his story."

They walked off together and very soon came upon a Gryphon† lying fast asleep in the sun. (If you don't

---

*Lewis Carroll's Mock Turtle has a turtle shell and front flippers combined with the head, hind hoofs, and tail of a calf. Mock turtle soup, a traditional dish made of veal, is meant to imitate green turtle soup.
†A Gryphon, a mythical beast, has the head, claws, and wings of an eagle, combined with the body, hind legs, and tail of a lion.

know what a Gryphon is, look at the picture.) "Up, lazy thing!" said the Queen, "and take this young lady to see the Mock Turtle. I must go back and see after some executions I have ordered!" And she walked off, leaving Alice alone with the Gryphon. Alice did not quite like the look of the creature, but on the whole she thought it would be quite as safe to stay with it as to go with that savage Queen.

The Gryphon sat up and rubbed its eyes: then it watched the Queen till she was out of sight: then it chuckled. "What fun!" said the Gryphon.

"What is?" said Alice.

"Why, *she*," said the Gryphon. "It's all her fancy that: they never executes nobody, you know.—Come on!"

"Everybody says 'come on!' here," thought Alice. "I never was so ordered about before in all my life, never!"

They had not gone far before they saw the Mock Turtle in the distance, sitting sad and lonely on a little ledge of rock, and, as they came nearer, Alice could hear him sighing as if his heart would break. She pitied him deeply. "What is his sorrow?" she asked the Gryphon. And the Gryphon answered, "It's all his fancy, that—just as the Queen pretends, so do he. He hasn't got no sorrow, you know."

So they went up to the Mock Turtle, who looked at them with large eyes full of tears, but said nothing.

"This here young lady," said the Gryphon, "she wants to know your story, she do."

"I'll tell it to her," said the Mock Turtle. "Sit down, both of you, and don't speak a word till I've finished."

So they sat down, and nobody spoke for some minutes. Alice thought to herself, "I don't see how he can *ever* finish, if he doesn't begin." But she waited patiently.

"Once," said the Mock Turtle at last, with a deep sigh,

He sobbed heavily for some time before continuing.

"I was a real Turtle." He sobbed heavily for some time before continuing. "When we were little, we went to school in the sea. The master was an old Turtle—we used to call him Tortoise—"

"Why did you call him Tortoise, if he wasn't one?" asked Alice.

"We called him *Tor*toise because he *taught* us," said the Mock Turtle. "Yes, we went to school in the sea, though you may not believe it—"

"I never said I didn't!" interrupted Alice.

"You did!" said the Mock Turtle.

"Hold your tongue!" added the Gryphon, before Alice could speak again. The Mock Turtle went on.

"We had the best of educations—in fact, we went to school every day—"

"And how many hours a day did you do lessons?" said Alice.

"Ten hours the first day," said the Mock Turtle: "nine the next, and so on."

"What a curious plan!" exclaimed Alice.

"That's the reason they're called lessons," the Gryphon remarked: "because they lessen from day to day."

This was quite a new idea to Alice, and she thought it over a little before she made her next remark. "Then the eleventh day must have been a holiday?"

"Of course it was," said the Mock Turtle.

"And how did you manage on the twelfth?" Alice went on.

"That's enough about lessons," the Gryphon interrupted. "Tell her something about the games now."

5. The Lobster-Quadrille*

The Mock Turtle sighed deeply, and drew the back of one flapper across his eyes. He looked at Alice and tried to speak, but, for a minute or two, sobs choked his voice. "Same as if he had a bone in his throat," said the Gryphon; and it set to work patting him on the back. At last the Mock Turtle recovered his voice, and, with tears running down his cheeks, he went on again:

"You may not have lived much under the sea—" ("I haven't," said Alice)—"and perhaps you were never even introduced to a lobster—" (Alice began to say, "I once tasted—" but checked herself and said, "No, never") "—so you can have no idea what a delightful thing a Lobster-Quadrille is!"

"No, indeed," said Alice. "What sort of a dance is it?"

"Why," said the Gryphon, "you first form into a line along the seashore—"

"Two lines!" cried the Mock Turtle. "Seals, turtles, salmon, and so on: then, when you've cleared all the jelly-fish out of the way—"

"*That* generally takes some time," interrupted the Gryphon.

"—you advance twice—"

"Each with a lobster as a partner!" cried the Gryphon.

---

*The quadrille was a difficult square dance that was popular when Lewis Carroll wrote this story.

56

"Of course," the Mock Turtle said: "advance twice, set to partners—"

"—change lobsters, and retire in the same order," continued the Gryphon.

"Then, you know," the Mock Turtle went on, "you throw the—"

"The lobsters!" shouted the Gryphon with a bound into the air.

"—as far out to sea as you can—"

"Swim after them!" screamed the Gryphon.

"Turn a somersault in the sea!" cried the Mock Turtle, capering wildly about.

"Change lobsters again!" yelled the Gryphon at the top of his voice.

"Back to land again, and—that's all the first figure," said the Mock Turtle, suddenly dropping his voice; and the two creatures, who had been jumping about like mad things all this time, sat down again very sadly and quietly and looked at Alice.

"It must be a very pretty dance," said Alice.

"Would you like to see a little of it?" said the Mock Turtle.

"Very much indeed," said Alice.

"Come, let's try the first figure!" said the Mock Turtle to the Gryphon. "We can do it without lobsters, you know. Which shall sing?"

"Oh, *you* sing," said the Gryphon. "I've forgotten the words."

So they began dancing round and round Alice, every now and then treading on her toes when they passed too close, and waving their forepaws to mark the time, when the Mock Turtle sang this, very slowly and sadly:

"Will you walk a little faster?" said a whiting to a snail,
"There's a porpoise close behind us, and he's treading on
*   my tail.*

See how eagerly the lobsters and the turtles all advance!
They are waiting on the shingle—will you come and join the
  dance?
  Will you, won't you, will you, won't you, will you join the
    dance?
  Will you, won't you, will you, won't you, won't you join the
    dance?"

"You can really have no notion how delightful it will be
"When they take us up and throw us, with the lobsters, out
  to sea!"
But the snail replied, "Too far, too far!" and gave a look
  askance—
Said he thanked the whiting* kindly, but he would not join
  the dance.
  Would not, could not, would not, could not, would not join
    the dance.
  Would not, could not, would not, could not, would not join
    the dance.

"What matters it how far we go?" his scaly friend replied.
"There is another shore, you know, upon the other side.
The further off from England, the nearer is to France—
Then turn not pale, beloved snail, but come and join the
  dance.
  Will you, won't you, will you, won't you, will you join the
    dance?
  Will you, won't you, will you, won't you, won't you join the
    dance?"

   "Thank you, it's a very interesting dance to watch,"
said Alice, feeling very glad that it was over at last: "and
I do so like that curious song about whiting!—If I'd been
the whiting, I'd have said to the porpoise, 'Keep back,
please! We don't want *you* with us!"

---

*A whiting, common in Europe, is an edible fish in the cod family.

"They had to have him with them," the Mock Turtle said. "No wise fish would go anywhere without a porpoise."

"Wouldn't it really?" said Alice.

"Of course not," said the Mock Turtle. "Why, if a fish came to *me*, and told me he was going on a journey, I should say, 'With what porpoise?'"

"Don't you mean 'purpose'?" said Alice.

"I mean what I say," the Mock Turtle replied.

The Gryphon interrupted, saying, "Come, let's hear some of *your* adventures."

"I could tell you my adventures—beginning from this morning," said Alice, "but it's no use going back to yesterday, because I was a different person then."

"Explain all that," said the Mock Turtle.

"No, no! The adventures first," said the Gryphon. "Explanations take such a dreadful long time."

So Alice began telling them her adventures from the time when she first saw the White Rabbit. She was a little nervous about it, just at first, the two creatures got so close to her, one on each side, and opened their eyes and mouths so *very* wide; but she gained courage as she went on. Her listeners were perfectly quiet till she got to the part about the Caterpillar.

"I think you'd better leave off," said the Gryphon, and Alice was only too glad to do so.

"Shall we try another figure of the Lobster-Quadrille?" the Gryphon went on. "Or would you like the Mock Turtle to sing you another song?"

"Oh, a song, please, if the Mock Turtle would be so kind," Alice replied.

"Hm!" said the Gryphon. "No accounting for tastes! Sing her 'Turtle Soup,' will you, old fellow?"

The Mock Turtle sighed very deeply, and began in a voice choked with sobs to sing this:

"Beautiful Soup, so rich and green,
Waiting in a hot tureen!
Who for such dainties would not stoop?
Soup of the evening, beautiful Soup!
Soup of the evening, beautiful Soup!
    Beau—ootiful Soo—oop!
    Beau—ootiful Soo—oop!
Soo—oop of the e—e—evening.
    Beautiful, beautiful Soup!

"Beautiful Soup! Who cares for fish,
Game, or any other dish?
Who would not give all else for two
pennyworth only of beautiful Soup?
    Beau—ootiful Soo—oop!
    Beau—ootiful Soo—oop!
Soo—oop of the e—e—evening.
    Beautiful, beauti—FUL SOUP!"

"Chorus again!" cried the Gryphon, and the Mock Turtle had just begun to repeat it, when a cry of "The trial's beginning!" was heard in the distance.

"Come on!" cried the Gryphon, and, taking Alice by the hand, it hurried off, without waiting for the end of the song.

"What trial is it?" Alice panted as she ran: but the Gryphon only answered, "Come on!" and ran the faster, while more and more faintly came, carried on the breeze that followed them, the melancholy words:

"Soo-oop of the e—e—evening,
    Beautiful, beautiful Soup!"

6. Who Stole the Tarts?

The King and Queen of Hearts were seated on their throne when they arrived, with a great crowd assembled about them—all sorts of little birds and beasts, as well as the whole pack of cards: the Knave was standing before them, in chains, with a soldier on each side to guard him; and near the King was the White Rabbit, with a trumpet in one hand, and a scroll in the other. In the very middle of the court was a table, with a large dish of tarts upon it: they looked so good, that it made Alice quite hungry to look at them—"I wish they'd get the trial done," she thought, "and hand round the refreshments!" But there seemed no chance of this; so she began looking at everything about her to pass away the time.

Alice had never been in a court of justice before, but she had read about them in books, and she was quite pleased to find that she knew the name of nearly everything there. "That's the judge," she said to herself, "because of his great wig."

The judge, by the way, was the King; and he wore his crown over the wig.

"And that's the jury-box," thought Alice; "and those twelve creatures" (she was obliged to say "creatures," you see, because some of them were animals, and some were birds), "I suppose they are the jurors."

The twelve jurors were all writing very busily on slates. "What are they doing?" Alice whispered to the Gryphon. "They can't have anything to put down yet, before the trial's begun."

The King and Queen of Hearts were seated on their throne when they arrived, with a great crowd assembled about them.

"They're putting down their names," the Gryphon whispered, "for fear they should forget them before the end of the trial."

"Stupid things!" Alice remarked in a loud voice, and the White Rabbit, hearing this, cried out, "Silence in the court!" The King put on his spectacles and looked round to make out who was talking.

Alice could see that all the jurors were writing down "Stupid things!" on their slates, and she could even make out that one of them didn't know how to spell "stupid," and that he had to ask his neighbor to tell him. "A nice mess their slates'll be in, before the trial's over!" thought Alice.

"Herald, read the accusation!" said the King.

At this, the White Rabbit blew three blasts on the trumpet, and then unrolled the scroll, and read as follows:—

"The Queen of Hearts, she made some tarts,
All on a summer day:
The Knave of Hearts, he stole those tarts
And took them quite away!"

"Consider your verdict," the King said to the jury.

"Not yet, not yet!" the Rabbit interrupted. "There's a great deal to come before that!"

"Call the first witness," said the King; and the White Rabbit blew three blasts on the trumpet, and called out, "First witness!"

The first witness was the Hatter. He came in with a teacup in one hand and a piece of bread-and-butter in the other. "I beg pardon, your Majesty," he began, "for bringing these in; but I hadn't quite finished my tea when I was sent for."

"Take off your hat," the King said.

"It isn't mine," said the Hatter.

At this, the White Rabbit blew three blasts on the trumpet.

"*Stolen!*" the King exclaimed, turning to the jury, who instantly made a note of the fact.

"I keep them to sell," the Hatter explained. "I've none of my own. I'm a hatter."

Here the Queen put on her spectacles, and began staring hard at the Hatter.

"Give your evidence," said the King, "and don't be nervous, or I'll have you executed on the spot."

This did not seem to relieve the witness's nervousness at all: he kept shifting from one foot to the other, looking worriedly at the Queen, and in his confusion he bit a large piece out of his teacup instead of the bread-and-butter.

Just at this moment Alice felt a very curious sensation, which puzzled her a great deal until she made out what it was: she was beginning to grow larger again, and she thought at first she would get up and leave the court; but on second thoughts she decided to remain where she was as long as there was room for her.

"I wish you wouldn't squeeze so," said the Dormouse, who was sitting next to her. "I can hardly breathe."

"I can't help it," said Alice. "I'm growing."

"You've no right to grow *here,*" said the Dormouse.

"Don't talk nonsense," said Alice. "You know you're growing too."

"Yes, but I grow at a reasonable pace," said the Dormouse: "not in that ridiculous fashion." And he got up very sulkily and crossed over to the other side of the court.

All this time the Queen had never left off staring at the Hatter, and the wretched man trembled so, that he shook off both his shoes.

"Give your evidence," the King repeated angrily, "or I'll have you executed, whether you are nervous or not."

The wretched man trembled so, that he shook off both his shoes.

"I'm a poor man, your Majesty," the Hatter began, in a trembling voice, "and I hadn't begun my tea—not above a week or so—and what with the bread-and-butter getting so thin—and the twinkling of the tea. Well, at any rate, the Dormouse said—" and the Hatter looked round to see if the Dormouse would deny saying it; but the Dormouse denied nothing, being fast asleep. "After that, I cut some more bread-and-butter—"

"But what did the Dormouse say?" one of the jurors asked.

"That I can't remember," said the Hatter.

"You *must* remember," remarked the King, "or I'll have you executed."

The miserable Hatter dropped his teacup and bread-and-butter, and went down on one knee. "I'm a poor man, your Majesty," he began.

"You're a very poor *speaker,*" said the King. "In any case, if that's all you know about it, you may go." The Hatter hurriedly left the court, without even waiting to put his shoes on.

"—and just take his head off outside," the Queen added to one of the officers, but the Hatter was out of sight before the officer could get to the door.

"Call the next witness!" said the King.

The next witness was the Duchess's cook. She carried the pepper-box in her hand, and Alice guessed who it was, even before she got into the court, by the way the people near the door began sneezing at once.

"Give your evidence," said the King.

"Shan't!" said the cook.

The King looked worriedly at the White Rabbit, who said, in a low voice, "Your Majesty must cross-examine this witness."

"Well, if I must, I must," the King said, and, after folding his arms and frowning at the cook, he said, in a deep voice, "What are tarts made of?"

"Pepper, mostly," said the cook.

"Molasses," said a sleepy voice behind her.

"Collar that Dormouse!" the Queen shrieked out. "Behead that Dormouse! Turn that Dormouse out of court! Pinch him! Off with his whiskers!"

For some minutes the whole court was in confusion, getting the Dormouse turned out, and, by the time they had settled down again, the cook had disappeared.

"Never mind!" said the King. "Call the next witness."
And he added to the Queen, "Really, my dear, *you* must
cross-examine the next witness. It quite makes my forehead ache!"

Alice watched the White Rabbit as he fumbled over
the list, feeling very curious to see what the next witness would be like, "—for they haven't got much evidence *yet*," she said to herself. Imagine her surprise,
when the White Rabbit read out, at the top of his shrill
little voice, the name "Alice!"

"Here!" cried Alice, quite forgetting in the flurry of
the moment how large she had grown in the last few
minutes, and she jumped up in such a hurry that she
tipped over the jurybox, upsetting all the jurors on to

She jumped up in such a hurry that she tipped over the jury-box.

the heads of the crowd below and there they lay sprawling about, reminding her very much of a bowl of goldfish she had accidentally upset the week before.

"Oh, I *beg* your pardon!" she exclaimed, and began picking them up again as quickly as she could, for the accident of the goldfish kept running in her head, and she had an idea that they must be collected at once and put back into the jury-box, or they would die.

"The trial cannot proceed," said the King, "until all the jurors are back in their proper places—*all*," he repeated, looking hard at Alice as he did so.

Alice looked at the jury-box, and saw that, in her haste, she had put the Lizard in head downwards, and the poor little thing was waving its tail about, being quite unable to move. She soon got it out again, and put it right.

As soon as the jury had a little recovered from the shock of being upset, and their slates and their pencils had been found and handed back to them, they set to work to write out a history of the accident, all except the Lizard, who seemed too much overcome to do anything but sit with its mouth open, gazing up into the roof of the court.

"What do you know about this business?" the King said to Alice.

"Nothing," said Alice.

"Nothing *whatever?*" asked the King.

"Nothing whatever," said Alice.

"That's very important," the King said, turning to the jury. They were just beginning to write this down on their slates, when the White Rabbit interrupted, "*Un*important, your Majesty means, of course."

"*Un*important, of course, I meant," the King said. He busily wrote in his notebook, then called out, "Silence!"

and read out from his book, "Rule Forty-two. *All persons more than a mile high must leave the court.*"

Everybody looked at Alice.

"*I'm* not a mile high," said Alice.

"You are," said the King.

"Nearly two miles high," added the Queen.

"Well, I shan't go, at any rate," said Alice. "Besides, that's not a regular rule: you invented it just now."

"It's the oldest rule in the book," said the King.

"Then it ought to be Rule One," said Alice.

The King turned pale, and shut his notebook hastily. "Consider your verdict," he said to the jury.

"There's more evidence to come yet, your Majesty," said the White Rabbit, jumping up in a great hurry. "This paper has just been picked up."

"What's in it?" said the Queen.

"I haven't opened it yet," said the White Rabbit, "but it seems to be a letter, written by the prisoner to—to somebody."

"It must have been that," said the King, "unless it was written to nobody, which isn't usual, you know."

"Who is it addressed to?" said one of the jurors.

"It isn't addressed at all," said the White Rabbit. "In fact, there's nothing written on the *outside*." He unfolded the paper as he spoke, and added, "It isn't a letter, after all: it's a set of verses."

"Are they in the prisoner's handwriting?" asked another of the jurors.

"No, they're not," said the White Rabbit, "and that's the oddest thing about it." (The jury all looked puzzled.)

"He must have imitated somebody's else's hand," said the King. (The jury all brightened up again.)

"Please, your Majesty," said the Knave. "I didn't write it, and they can't prove that I did: there's no name signed at the end."

"If you didn't sign it," said the King, "that only makes the matter worse. You *must* have meant some mischief, or else you'd have signed your name like an honest man."

There was a general clapping of hands at this: it was the first really clever thing the King had said that day.

"That *proves* his guilt, of course," said the Queen: "so, off with—"

"It doesn't prove anything of the sort!" said Alice. "Why, you don't even know what they're about!"

"Read them," said the King.

The White Rabbit put on his spectacles. "Where shall I begin, your Majesty?" he asked.

"Begin at the beginning," said the King, "and go on till you come to the end: then stop."

There was dead silence in the court, while the White Rabbit read out these verses:

> *"They told me you had been to her,*
> *And mentioned me to him;*
> *She gave me a good character,*
> *But said I could not swim.*
>
> *He sent them word I had not gone*
> *(We know it to be true);*
> *If she should push the matter on,*
> *What would become of you?*
>
> *I gave her one, they gave him two,*
> *You gave us three or more;*
> *They all returned from him to you,*
> *Though they were mine before.*
>
> *If I or she should chance to be*
> *Involved in this affair,*
> *He trusts to you to set them free,*
> *Exactly as we were.*

My notion was that you had been
   (Before she had this fit)
An obstacle that came between
   Him, and ourselves, and it.

Don't let him know she liked them best,
   For this must ever be
A secret, kept from all the rest,
   Between yourself and me."

"That's the most important piece of evidence we've heard yet," said the King, rubbing his hands; "so now let the jury—"

"If any one of them can explain it," said Alice (she had grown so large in the last few minutes that she wasn't a bit afraid of interrupting him), "I'll give him sixpence. *I* don't believe there's an atom of meaning in it."

The jury all wrote down, on their slates, "*She* doesn't believe there's an atom of meaning in it," but none of them attempted to explain the paper.

"If there's no meaning in it," said the King, "that saves a world of trouble, you know, as we needn't try to find any. And yet I don't know," he went on, spreading out the verses on his knee, and looking at them with one eye: "I seem to see some meaning in them, after all. '— *said I could not swim—*' you can't swim, can you?" he added, turning to the Knave.

The Knave shook his head sadly. "Do I look like it?" he said. (Which he certainly did *not,* being made entirely of cardboard.)

"All right, so far," said the King; and he went on muttering over the verses to himself: "'*We know it to be true*'—that's the jury, of course—'*If she should push the matter on*'—that must be the Queen—'*What would become of you?*'—What, indeed!—'*I gave her one, they gave him two'*—why, that must be what he did with the tarts, you know—"

"But it goes on, *'they all returned from him to you,'*" said Alice.

"Why, there they are!" said the King triumphantly, pointing to the tarts on the table. "Nothing can be clearer than that. Then again—*'before she had this fit'*—you never had fits, my dear, I think?" he said to the Queen.

"Never!" said the Queen.

"Then the words don't *fit* you," said the King. "Now, let the jury consider their verdict."

"No, no!" said the Queen. "Sentence first—verdict afterwards."

"Stuff and nonsense!" said Alice. "The idea of having the sentence first."

"Hold your tongue!" said the Queen.

"I won't!" said Alice.

"Off with her head!" the Queen shouted. But nobody moved.

"Who cares for *you*?" said Alice (she had grown to her full size by this time.) "You're nothing but a pack of cards!"

At this the whole pack rose up into the air, and came flying down upon her; she gave a little scream, half of fright and half of anger, and tried to beat them off, and found herself lying on the bank, with her head in the lap of her sister, who was gently brushing away some dead leaves that had fluttered down from the trees upon her face.

"Wake up, Alice dear!" said her sister. "Why, what a long sleep you've had!"

"Oh, I've had such a curious dream!" said Alice. And she told her sister, as well as she could remember them, all these strange Adventures of hers that you

*At this the whole pack rose up into the air,
and came flying down upon her.*

have just been reading about; and, when she had finished, her sister kissed her, and said, "It *was* a curious dream, dear, certainly; but now run in to your tea: it's getting late." So Alice got up and ran off, thinking while she ran, as well she might, what a wonderful dream it had been.

But her sister sat still just as she left her, leaning her head on her hand, watching the setting sun, and thinking of little Alice and all her wonderful Adventures, till she too began dreaming after a fashion, and this was her dream:—

First, she dreamed about little Alice herself: once again the tiny hands were clasped upon her knee, and the bright eager eyes were looking up into hers—she could hear the very tones of her voice, and see that odd little toss of her head to keep back the wandering hair that *would* always get into her eyes—and still as she listened, or seemed to listen, the whole place around her became alive with the strange creatures of her little sister's dream.

The long grass rustled at her feet as the White Rabbit hurried by—the frightened Mouse splashed his way through the neighboring pool—she could hear the rattle of the teacups as the March Hare and his friends shared their never-ending meal, and the shrill voice of the Queen ordering off her unfortunate guests to execution—once more the pig-baby was sneezing on the Duchess's knee, while plates and dishes crashed around it—once more the shriek of the Gryphon and the squeaking of the Lizard's slate-pencil filled the air, mixed up with the distant sob of the miserable Mock Turtle.

So she sat on, with closed eyes, and half believed herself in Wonderland, though she knew she had but to open them again, and all would change to simple reality—the grass would be only rustling in the wind, and the pool rippling to the waving of the reeds—the rattling teacups would change to tinkling sheep-bells, and the Queen's shrill cries to the voice of the shepherd-boy—and the sneeze of the baby, the shriek of the Gryphon, and all the other strange noises, would change (she knew) to the confused sounds of the busy farmyard—while the mooing of the cattle in the distance would take the place of the Mock Turtle's heavy sobs.

Lastly, she pictured to herself how this same little sister of hers would, in the after-time, be herself a grown woman; and how she would keep, through all her older years, the simple and loving heart of her childhood; and how she would gather about her other little children, and make *their* eyes bright and eager with many a strange tale, perhaps even with the dream of Wonderland of long ago; and how she would feel with all their simple sorrows, and find a pleasure in all their simple joys, remembering her own child-life, and the happy summer days.

THE END